Red Planet Refugees

LIANA BROOKS

OTHER WORKS

Fey Lights
Prime Sensations

HEROES AND VILLAINS

Even Villains Fall In Love
Even Villains Go To The Movies
Even Villains Have Interns
Even Villains Play The Hero (books 1 – 3 omnibus)

TIME AND SHADOWS MYSTERIES

The Day Before
Convergence Point
Decoherence

FLEET OF MALIK

Bodies In Motion
Change of Momentum
For Every Action (forthcoming)

Find other works by the author at
www.lianabrooks.com

Red Planet Refugees

INKLET #14

LIANA BROOKS

Inkprint PRESS

www.inkprintpress.com

Print ISBN: 978-1-925825-13-8
eBook ISBN: 9781386050827

www.inkprintpress.com

National Library of Australia Cataloguing-in-Publication Data
Liana Brooks 1982 –
Red Planet Refugees
34 p.
ISBN: 978-1-925825-13-8
Inkprint Press, Canberra, Australia
1. Fiction—Short Stories 2. Fiction—Science Fiction 3. Fiction—Science Fiction—Space Exploration

First Print Edition: July 2019
Cover design © Inkprint Press
Interior art © Amy Laurens

RED PLANET
REFUGEES

Blue lightning arched through red clouds boiling on the horizon. The sun hung low, a reminder of the day to come, a reminder of searing heat and the outpost's dwindling water supply. I pulled another shirt off of the line and risked a peek at the dark horizon.

Nothing.

The distant galaxies were too faint to be seen, and there were no near stars. We were the last outposts, the last human refuge before nothingness. But I didn't care about that; I was looking for the ice ship.

Every year it was a race. The original colonists were left with a single vessel to conduct basic observations and experiments. When the domes failed, that single ship moved my ancestors to the outpost monitoring the storm world. And now that one ship collected ice from the rings farther out to give us the water we needed to survive.

I didn't expect them today, or tomorrow, or even soon. We still had six months' worth of water left, if nothing went wrong. We could survive that.

But I still looked.

Taking the last shirt off the line, I waved to my neighbor. The gray-haired matron was the eldest of her small clan and the only one I knew on sight. The rest she kept cloistered inside their dome, safe from the radiation of the sun. I didn't have anyone protecting me. I didn't have anyone to protect. My only brother left after his wife and son died. My parents died years before that in a rationing scare; we'd survived while they wasted away from dehydration.

Instinctively, I checked the water levels as I walked inside. All the monitors showed the tank three-quarters full. Good enough for now.

I turned on the radio as I dumped clean linens on my make-shift bed and debated hanging my last few wet things on the line.

"Good morning everyone! This is Joe and Jo! Twenty-three minutes to full sunrise and it's already one hundred and ten outside. Looks like it'll be a hot one!" Joe yelled through the radio.

His wife, Jo, came on with a higher-pitched but equally-enthusiastic tone. "Hiya folks! Are you all ready for the day? Is your laundry in? Your dishes washed? Great! Because we have a full load of fun for you!"

I tossed my last suits into my basket and walked back outside. They were mostly dry and if I pulled them in within an hour, nothing would burn.

Coming back, I sealed the door behind me as the Hilda's Children's Chorus sang the wake-up song. The radio chimed and the family in charge of monitoring water gave their daily report.

Everything was fine, water levels were great, consumption was slightly up in the greenhouse because of the new seedlings being at 'that stage', but things were expected to level out in about seventeen days.

The radio chimed again and Jo cut in. "That was great kids! I'm glad to hear you so perky on this hot, hot day!"

"And thank you to the Dugroot clan for watching our water supplies. It's a grave responsibility," Joe said, giving the word 'grave' extra emphasis, "and for the last eight generations the Dugroots have proven they're willing to sacrifice to see the rising generation watered."

"Now that we've had the good news, let's try some bad news!" Jo enthused.

"Over to you, Jessa!" Joe said.

The radio chimed as I slid into my usual seat and pulled my microphone close. I smiled just like my brother taught me and started talking. "It's a wonderful morning over here at Far Out Skywatch and let me tell you, folks, there is nothing to see. Not a blessed blip on the radar screen. We are well and truly alone. But that's the bad news; let's try some more good news!"

"You have good news?" Jo cut in from the radio's main control panel.

"Believe it or not, Jo, I do!" I said, matching her enthusiasm. "Last dark we got a call from the ice ship. They're doing well and they sent their letters home." I pulled out my notepad and started reading. "Johnny sends May his love and says he hopes to be home in time for the baby. Trounce says 'hiya' to Ma and his brother. Matthew wants to let his clan know he's learning piloting and catching now, and making them proud. And young Egglebert, who's on his first tour, sends to say 'hiya' to all the folks at home, the view is great, and he's loving everything, and then the captain cut him off." I paused, imaging the clans gathered around the radio for our communal morning show laughing.

"The good Captain Tryer says to tell y'all that the ship's fuel is at eighty-seven percent and they're catching extra ice with the new nets that we rigged last season. Everything is in good working order; food supplies and morale are high. They expect to spend another twelve weeks catching and hope to bring home extra water this season.

"That's all I got, folks. This is Far Out Skywatch, if something happens

I'll let you know!"

Jo and Joe took over as I switched off my radio. As I folded clothes and bathed, Jo and Joe prattled on, telling jokes, discussing books, and asking questions of the various clans.

As they started the 'Too Hot to Talk' song, I pulled on my shoes to get the last of the laundry off the line.

I laughed at the stale jokes. There were only seventeen families that had survived the past two-hundred-plus years of hardships; eventually we'd run out of things to say. But Jo and Joe kept morale high while we waited each season for crops to grow in our dimly-lit gardens and the ship to return with ice, all the while praying to some deity none of us knew that one day the nations that had sent our forefathers out would come back to rescue us.

I paused by the sealed door and touched the little calendar that my father had left. Eighty-eight. Eighty-eight seasons until inbreeding, faulty technology, or lack of food killed us. The first refugees to arrive at the outpost had calculated how long they thought we could survive and made the calendar. By now most people had thrown theirs away in despair, but I kept ours, carefully removing one number each season, wondering if my ancestors who had carved the 324 pieces of wood ever imagined that we would still be on this planet when the wood ran out.

The radio chimed. I looked over my shoulder, frowning.

I really needed to get my laundry in before the temperatures soared, but it was rude to keep someone waiting.

The radio chimed again.

With a shrug I walked over to the radio station, my finger tracing down the line of lights to see who was trying to contact me.

Red four. Who was red four?

I hit the red light and my radar screen lit up green and black. I blinked as the radar blipped.

A blip?

What did that mean? My brother had taught me maintenance but he never mentioned blips.

I hustled to the back room where we kept the ancestors' books, diaries, and valuables tucked away for a future generation of refugees. I dragged my finger across the titles, trying to read fast enough to find the book I wanted in a hurry. There, written in Geek, a technician's manual for the radar array.

I pulled it down and scanned for a picture that matched my blipping radar. I found it a quarter of the way through the book. The caption read, 'Long Distance Array Radar Reading An Incoming Vessel.'

My heart stuttered as I skimmed the chapter. The black and green radar was the long-distance, deep-space radar, entirely different from the familiar red land-tracker that followed the ice ship landing.

I ran back to my radio and slammed my palm on the call button. "Hiya, folks, this is Far Out Skywatch and, um, according to the technician's manual I'm reading, the deep-space array has been activated by a, a..." I sucked in a long breath and spat out, "by an incoming hyperspace vessel that isn't broadcasting the pre-programmed security clearance.

"Folks." I grinned wildly. "We have visitors."

THE MAKING OF
RED PLANET REFUGEES

Even though *Red Planet Refugees* comes after *Seventy* in the canon time-line, this story came first.

It was a blistering hot Texas summer. The temperatures hadn't dropped below 100F (38C) in ninety days. Even over night the heat was oppressive. I had no working dryer at the time, so I was going out to hang laundry every morning, trying to beat the worst of the sun's heat.

And a story was born.

DOWNLOAD YOUR FREE EBOOK

When you buy a print book from Inkprint Press, we like to say THANK YOU by offering you the ebook for free!

Please head to www.inkprintpress.com/inklets/14/ and the use the coupon INK14 to get your copy of this Inklet in epub AND mobi today!
(Coupon will only work once.)

Read more by Liana Brooks!

PRIME SENSATIONS

"Unidentified vessel, we are Waste Hauler 133 out of Darrian 6. We carry no trade or crew," the ship's AI droned in a bored monotone.

Lana dropped into the waste hauler's modified control booth and took over. "Unidentified vessel, be advised. I steer like a drunken moose, alter your course." The reverb over the frequently patched comm lines made her sound like an old man with a lifelong bitter-root habit.

Sweat dripped down her nose. The waste hauler had a hull thirty years older than she was, and an environmental system older than that. It had survived two major system wars by being too worthless to target. And Lana was well aware that, as a debtor working off her ransom to the Iloni nation, she was slightly less valuable than the ship.

The comm crackled and she thought she heard the word "boarding."

"Unidentified vessel," she replied, "I am deaf and blind. I give you no authorization to come near this vessel. If you keep to your projected course I will have no choice but to heartlessly smash your hull because of physics."

The other ship tried to respond.

Lana grimaced and tried to compensate for the ancient communications array. "Mass times acceleration, unidentified vessel. I can't slow down in time."

"Waste Hauler 133, this is the *Marsail* out of Port Tael, flying the flag of the Exaner Confederation. Prepare to be boarded."

Black holes and dark nights! Port Tael was a pirate station, taken by the outer rim unification during the Apex

War, and currently under stars-only-knew which warlord.

She leaned against the rough metal of the control booth. They probably wanted to pick over the hauler for parts. Stars knew there was enough wreckage welded in to rebuild a fleet. She should probably get dressed.

Lana sniffed her armpit. Maybe a shower was in order. And clothes. And snacks. The *Marsail* wouldn't cross paths with her hauler for a few more hours, and it was the most exciting thing to happen since she'd been taken as a prisoner of war three years ago.

A shower and change of clothes later, Lana watched as the *Marsail* managed to land on the bulky waste hauler with a finesse Lana would have envied a few years ago, back when she'd thought her rift rat piloting skills would be enough to win the attention she craved.

It never had.

She tossed a boiled nut into her mouth and watched the pirate crew's slow progress through the hull. If there'd been someone to bet against, she would have wagered they'd go for the hard metals compartment, maybe grab some radiated shielding or a new engine converter.

Her second bet was the food waste department, where they might try panning for seeds. Not that it would do them any good—the Iloni poisoned the food waste to ensure the vegetation of Darrian 6 wasn't sold on the black market—but they were welcome to try.

The enemy ship latched on like a leech and sliced through her hull. The crew moved methodically toward the control deck.

If she'd had a weapon, she would have gone out to meet them. The only gear worth having was the bits she'd salvaged. Not enough to build a shuttle, not yet, but in another year or three she'd have a means of escape. If they took that...

Lana eyed the console and considered the maneuvers she'd need to shake the smaller ship off. Scraping them against the mine corridor that kept her from diverting off course sounded promising.

She was running over the possible course corrections needed when someone banged on the door of the control booth.

"Pilot?" The person hammered on the door again. "Waste Hauler Pilot, open this door."

She raised an eyebrow and grabbed another boiled nut. Telling the intruder she'd survived far worse than they could dish out was a waste of oxygen. Right now, she was breathing. If that changed in the next few minutes, no one was going to care, least of all her.

"Open this door or we will open it for you."

"Be my guest."

"Stand back."

She looked around at the cramped booth, a cylinder of buttons, viewing screens, and control panels. Given enough time and the right tools, she could rip out the main radar and stuff herself into the box, but that would take at least an hour.

The door in front of her radiated heat.

Lana lifted the chair that had long ago rusted loose just in time to prevent hot metal shrapnel from hitting her face.

"Hi." She set the chair down so she could look into the black faceplate of her attacker. With a smile, she slapped the panic button that sent the waste hauler into a death spiral, alarm beacons screaming. "Iloni forces will be here within the hour. Do you want to shoot me now, or later?" The increased gravity of the spiral pulled at her. For a moment it looked like her attacker planned on retreating. She winked at the black face mask. "Pretty girl got your tongue?"

The invader pushed past her, boots scrapping along the floor, and fumbled to hit the bypass code with large hands. "You think I don't know that trick?"

"You think I care what you know?"

The faceplate cleared as he turned to her. And Lana found herself staring into the shocked eyes of Kaleb Hath— the man who'd left her for dead.

Lana's nails bit into her palms as her fists clenched. "Commander Hath," she said, "if I'd known it was you, I would have vented my oxygen an hour ago."

Keep reading! Head to:
http://www.lianabrooks.com/books/short-stories/
to buy your copy now!

ABOUT THE AUTHOR

LIANA BROOKS was born on the planet Earth in the Sol System and, despite an uncanny knack for understanding spaceships, it seems probable that she is at least mostly human. She currently resides on the Pacific coast of North America with her family and her pet fish.

Brooks has written the popular *Time and Shadows Mysteries* series about clones and the dangers of time travel; the *Fleet of Malik* series of connected sci-fi romances about re-building after a decades-long war; and the cult-following *Heroes and Villains* series of superhero romances.

You can find out more about Liana at her website, www.lianabrooks.com.

INKLETS

Collect them all! Released on the 1st and 15th of each month.

INKLET #007
SEVENTY
LIANA BROOKS

INKLET #008
A Final Request for Mercy
AMY LAURENS

INKLET #009
the kitten psychologist
vs.
the kitten's owners
THEA VAN DIEPEN

INKLET #010
Answer the Question
AMY LAURENS

INKLET #011
Happily, Red
AMY LAURENS

INKLET #012
the kitten psychologist
tries to be patient
through email
THEA VAN DIEPEN

INKLET #013
DRAGON TUESDAY
AMY LAURENS

INKLET #014
RED PLANET REFUGEES
LIANA BROOKS

INKLET #015
the kitten psychologist &
What The Kitten Did
THEA VAN DIEPEN

INKLET #016
Cherry Blossom
AMY LAURENS

INKLET #017
Alone
AMY LAURENS

INKLET #018
the kitten psychologist
& The Kitten
Come To A Conclusion
THEA VAN DIEPEN

INKLET #019
LEVEL NINE
LIANA BROOKS

INKLET #020
To Dust
AMY LAURENS

INKLET #021
Interchange
AMY LAURENS

INKLET #022
Emalia's Lanterns
LIANA BROOKS

INKLET #023
Dear Santa
AMY LAURENS

INKLET #024
The Quilt-Maker's Scrap
AMY L. LAURENS